This igloo book belongs to:

....

igloobooks

Published in 2018
Igloo Books Ltd
Cottage Farm
Sywell
NN6 0BJ
www.igloobooks.com

HUN001 0618
2 4 6 8 10 9 7 5 3 1
ISBN 978-1-78810-872-0

Written by Xanna Chown
Illustrated by James Newman Gray

Cover designed by Sacha Robinson-Forster and Jason Shortland
Interiors designed by Jason Shortland
Edited by Kathryn Beer

Printed and manufactured in China

My First Treasury of
Snowy Stories

igloobooks

Contents

Little Bunny's Snowman

Little Bunny was very excited. "There's snow in the garden," he squeaked.
"Let's have a competition!" shouted his big sister. "The best snowman wins."
"Little Bunny's too small to make a snowman," laughed his big brother.
"No I'm not," said Little Bunny, crossly.

Little Bunny watched his brother scoop up the snow
with his paws, pat it into a ball and roll it along the ground.
The little snowball got bigger and bigger until it was
almost the size of Little Bunny's head.

7

"That looks easy," said Little Bunny. He scooped up some snow and started to roll. Whoops! He tripped over and the snowball fell to pieces. "Oh, dear," said his brother. "You're no good at making a big snowball."

Little Bunny's sister had made her own snowman and was decorating it. She wrapped a purple scarf around his neck and gave him an old, woolly hat to wear. "You can give him this carrot for a nose if you like," said Little Bunny's sister.

Little Bunny tried to press the carrot gently onto the snowman's head to give him a nose. He pushed a bit too hard and the snowman's head wobbled this way and that. "Little Bunny!" shouted his sister. "You're ruining my snowman!"

"Perhaps I am too small to make a snowman," thought Little Bunny.
He walked away sadly, but he wasn't looking where he was going.
THUMP! He bumped into the bottom of a tree. FLUMP!
All the snow from the branches fell on top of him!

Little Bunny was covered in a blanket of cold, wet snow.
He ran back to tell his brother and sister what had
happened, but when they saw him, they looked scared.
"Help! Help!" shouted his brother. "It's a walking snowman!"

Little Bunny shook off the snow and it flew all over the garden.
His brother and sister laughed when they saw that he was the snowman.
"Little Bunny," said his brother, "you've won the competition."
"Yes," giggled his sister, "you made the best snowman by far!"

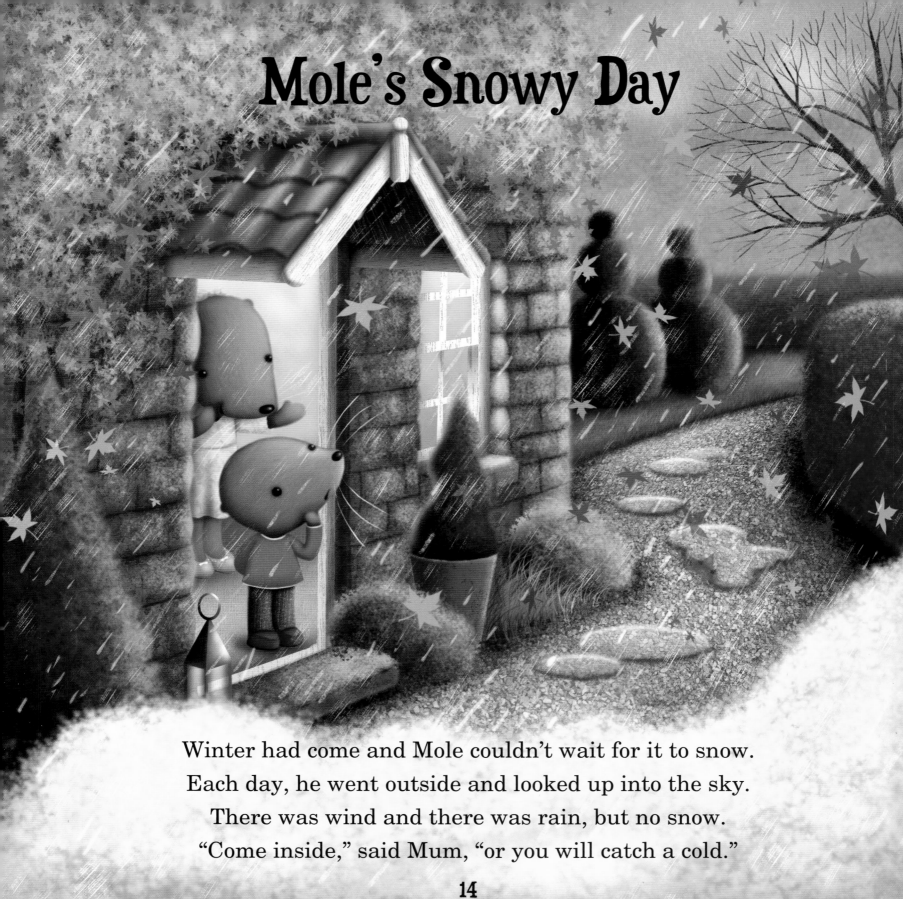

Mole's Snowy Day

Winter had come and Mole couldn't wait for it to snow.
Each day, he went outside and looked up into the sky.
There was wind and there was rain, but no snow.
"Come inside," said Mum, "or you will catch a cold."

Then, one day, Mole woke up and opened his curtains.
"It's snowing!" he cried, but his voice was a bit croaky.
Mole's throat was sore and his head hurt. Suddenly, he
gave a big sneeze. Atishoo! Mole had caught a cold.

Downstairs, the doorbell rang. Mole's friends had come to call for him. "It's snowing!" cried Bunny. "Come out and play." Mole snuffled and sniffled and gave a big sneeze. "I can't," he said sadly, "I've got a cold."

Mole's mum tucked him back in bed. "It's not fair," said
Mole, sniffling sadly, "I want to play in the snow, too."
He gave one big, "Atishoo!" and snuggled down for
a snuffly sleep. Just then, Mum had an idea.

"I know how Mole can play in the snow," said Mum to
Bunny and Squirrel. Mum got lots of white tissue paper.
"Follow me," she said, placing the paper and scissors on the table.
They all gathered round and Mum told them what to do.

When Mole woke up, he found paper snowflakes around
his bedroom. "Surprise!" shouted Mum, Bunny and Squirrel.
"We made it snow for you!" Mole felt much better because now it
was snowing inside, too. "It's double the snowy fun!" he cried.

Snow Stories

"Let's not build a snowman," Little Bear said.
"I've got a much better plan instead!
We'll make a snow spaceship and travel to Mars.
Let's zoom round the Moon and then visit the stars."

"Let's play snow pirates," Little Bear roared.
"We'll go on a snow ship with treasure aboard.
We won't mind if the weather is icy and cold,
As long as we have all our huge bags of gold."

"Let's make a snow castle," Little Bear cried.
"We'll have turrets and thrones and a moat that is wide.
We'll be kings and queens for the whole of the day.
People will have to do whatever we say!"

"Let's be snow explorers," Little Bear smiled.
"We can search for ice monsters that live in the wild.
We'll look for their footprints and track them and then,
Tomorrow we'll do it all over again."

Winter Clothes

Badger couldn't wait to go to the park to play spacemen.
"Wrap up warm," said his dad. Badger tried to wrap up warm,
but his coat was too small, there were holes in his boots
and he could only find one glove!

"Oh, dear," laughed Badger's dad. "We'd better go and buy you some
new clothes." Badger stamped crossly all the way to the shops.
He didn't want new clothes. He wanted to whizz down the
big slide and pretend he was shooting into a Moon crater.

Suddenly, it started to rain. "We'll have to get the boots first or your feet will get wet," said Badger's dad. They stopped at the shoe shop and bought a pair of shiny, gold boots.
"Can we go to the park now, Dad?" asked Badger. "I want to be a spaceman!"

"We need to get you a coat," said Badger's dad. Badger tried on a
shiny, silver coat. "Let's get the matching trousers, too."
They were covered in a pattern of sparkling purple stars.
"Now can we go to the park so I can be a spaceman?" asked Badger.

"You still need some gloves," said Badger's dad. Badger tried on spotty gloves, fluffy gloves and then, he found a pair of sparkly, golden gloves. "These ones are perfect," said Badger's dad. Badger mumbled in agreement. "Please, Dad. Can we go to the park now?" he asked, running out of the shop.

28

"Wait," said his dad, smiling. "There's one more thing you need."
In the toy shop, they found a plastic spaceman's helmet.
Badger put it on and looked at himself in the mirror.
"Wow!" shouted Badger, excitedly. "I look just like a spaceman!"

Badger and his dad had finally reached the park.
Badger's friends were already there, swaying on the swings.
Badger jumped towards them like he was walking on the Moon.
"You look amazing!" they cried. "Let's pretend the slide is a
rocket ship! The climbing frame can be the Moon!"

"Three… two… one… blast-off!" yelled Badger,
as he zoomed down the slide and into outer space.
"Badger looks like a real spaceman," his friends shouted.
"I feel like one, too," said Badger. "Thanks for my new clothes, Dad."

31

Seal's Icy Adventure

Seal was going on an underwater adventure.
She dived into the icy sea with a splash!
"Don't swim too far," warned her mother.
"I won't," promised Seal, but she couldn't wait to explore.

Seal saw some tiny lights blinking in the water below her.
She darted down to take a closer look. It was a group of
jellyfish glowing in the light. They waved hello to Seal with
their wiggly tentacles.

Suddenly, the sea went dark. An enormous whale was
blocking the light! Seal waved a flipper and the whale
waved back. It was the biggest animal she had ever seen.
"I can't wait to tell Mum," she thought.

Seal flicked her tail, flapped her fins and carried on exploring.
She wanted to find out what lived at the bottom of the ocean.
A family of crabs were walking sideways along a craggy rock.
They smiled at her then scuttled away, clicking their claws.

Suddenly, Seal saw a sunken ship lying in the sand.
It was old and dark and Seal felt a bit scared. Whoosh!
An octopus wriggled out of a porthole, making her squeal.
"I've had enough exploring for today," gasped Seal.

Seal swam back up to the surface as quickly as she could.
Her mum was waiting by the ice hole to give Seal a big hug.
"I've had an amazing adventure," said Seal, happily,
"but I'm glad to be back home again."

I Love Winter

When winter comes, I play outside because it's so much fun.
It's easy to keep warm and snug when you play games and run.

I don't mind if it rains because I've got my boots to wear.
I jump in muddy puddles and splash water everywhere.

If it's icy, I can slip and slide along the path.
I pretend that I'm a skating star to make my brothers laugh.

When playtime's over for the day, there's just one place for me.
I'm snug and warm inside my house, just where I want to be.

The Perfect Present

It was the morning of Hedgehog's birthday and more than anything in the world, she wanted it to snow. She jumped out of bed and flung open the curtains, but there was no snow.

"It's not snowing," she said, walking downstairs sadly.

"Don't worry," said her dad. "We'll have a snow party whatever the weather."

Later that day, the doorbell went. DING-DONG! Hedgehog's friends were arriving for the party. "Dad's made loads of food for us," she said, letting them in. There were snowflake biscuits, big mounds of wobbly jelly and bowls full of yummy sweets. Hedgehog and her friends piled up their plates with all the delicious food.

"Let's play Pass the Parcel now," said Hedgehog. They passed around a snowball-shaped gift and ripped off layers of wrapping paper. "Wow! A beautiful snow globe," said Mouse, tearing off the last layer. Next, they played Musical Snowmen. They jumped around when the music was playing and stood as still as they could when it stopped.

Then, Hedgehog's mother brought out the birthday cake. It looked
just like a snowy forest, with white icing and sugar trees.
"Make a wish!" everyone called. Hedgehog shut her eyes,
blew out the candles and wished really hard.

"What shall we do next?" asked Hedgehog. "We've eaten
all the party food and played all the party games already!"
"Why don't you look outside?" said her dad, with a smile on his face.
Hedgehog and her friends ran to the window and looked outside.
The garden was covered in a thick blanket of snow.

"It's snowing!" cried Hedgehog, as she ran into the garden with her friends.
They had fun making snowmen and throwing snowballs all afternoon.
"This is the best snow party ever!" shouted her friends.
"I know," sighed Hedgehog, happily. "My birthday wish really did come true."

The Penguin Games

Little Penguin was practising for the Snowy Peaks ice-skating competition. He slid slowly across the ice, slipped and landed on his bottom with a thump. "I'll never be as good as everyone else," he sighed as he watched the other skaters whirl and twirl on the ice. "I'm just too clumsy."

The competition was about to begin and Little Penguin waited patiently in line with the other skaters. Big Penguin whooshed over the ice, leapt high in the air and landed perfectly. The crowd erupted with clapping and cheers.

Next, Fluffy Penguin dashed past. She darted around the
ice and started to spin in a circle. Round and round she
whirled, faster and faster, until Little Penguin felt dizzy.
The crowd gasped in amazement.

Dotty Penguin was the final skater to go before Little Penguin.
Her skates sparkled as she danced beautifully and zoomed across the ice.
Finally, it was Little Penguin's turn to skate. He stepped nervously
onto the ice and carefully made his way to the centre.

Rainy Day Treasure

Chipmunk was spending a rainy day at Grandma's house.
It was too wet to play outside, so Grandma said, "Let's have
a treasure hunt!" Grandma read the first clue aloud.
"TO FIND A CLUE, LOOK IN A SHOE."

Chipmunk scampered into the hall and started to search.
She tipped up big shoes and little shoes, wellies and
fluffy slippers. A piece of paper fluttered to the ground and
she scooped it up. It was the next clue!

"WHO'S IN THE BATH? TRY NOT TO LAUGH," read Chipmunk. She raced upstairs to the bathroom. Two funny, plastic ducks were sitting in the bathtub. Chipmunk giggled as she pulled a piece of paper out of one of the ducks' beaks.

"I'M UNDER YOUR HEAD, WHEN YOU'RE IN BED," she said aloud.
Chipmunk scrambled onto Grandma's bed, Boing! It was very bouncy.
Grandma's frilly pillows fell on the floor and Chipmunk saw the next clue.

"LOOK IN A TRUNK, LITTLE CHIPMUNK," read Chipmunk.
She rushed to the attic and searched through a huge box full of
old clothes. She found a big, flowery hat and tried it on.
The clue fell out onto her nose!

The final clue said, "SNIFF THE AIR WELL, WHAT CAN YOU SMELL?"
Chipmunk noticed a delicious smell coming from the kitchen.
She ran downstairs and saw Grandma holding a tray of warm biscuits.
"Well done!" cried Grandma, smiling. "You've found the treasure!"

Winter Knitting

Fox's mummy loves to knit. She curls up in her chair.
She makes socks and scarves and hats for little Fox to wear.

Sometimes the socks come out too big and the hats come out too tight.
Sometimes the scarves are just too long. It's hard to get it right.

Most of them fit perfectly and then his mum is done.
Then, Fox is snuggly and warm and ready for wintery fun.

When the garden fills with snow, Fox runs to play out there.
All the clothes that don't fit him, his snowman loves to wear!

Sledging Trouble

Hoppy Bunny had a brand new sledge. It was shiny and
green and she knew it would whizz down the slopes.
"Can I come sledging, too?" asked Fluffy Bunny.
"No," said Hoppy. "No one can ride my sledge except me."

Hoppy dragged her sledge outside. Cat waved at her from his garden. "Are you going sledging?" called Cat. Hoppy nodded. "Can I come?" "No," said Hoppy. "You don't have a sledge and I'm not sharing mine."

When Hoppy reached the bottom of the hill, she saw Mouse.
"Shall I help you pull your sledge to the top?" asked Mouse.
"Then we can zoom down together."
"No," said Hoppy. "I want to ride all by myself."

Hoppy dragged her sledge to the top of the hill on her own.
It was hard work with no one to help her. She reached the top
of the hill and turned the sledge to face the slope. All of a sudden,
the sledge began to slide down the hill, all by itself.

"Oh, no!" cried Hoppy as she watched the sledge whizz away.
She began to run down the hill after it, but she slipped
and tumbled into the snow. She came to a stop by her
sledge near the bottom of the hill.

Just then, Hoppy saw Fluffy playing in the snow with Cat and Mouse. They were having lots of fun. Hoppy felt sad. "Sledging's no fun on my own," she said. Hoppy jumped on the sledge and slid down the hill to where the three friends were playing.

"I'm sorry I didn't want to share," said Hoppy.
"Do you still want to come sledging?"
"Of course we do!" they said together. The friends
raced to the top of the slope. Hoppy and Fluffy sat on the
sledge and held on tightly as Cat gave them a big push.

The friends spent the whole afternoon having fun.
They took it in turns to pull the sledge up the hill and
zoom down again. Hoppy was glad she'd finally decided
to share her new sledge and her friends were, too!

Frosty Morning

It was a cold, winter's morning and Squirrel was tucked up in bed.
"Let's play outside," said Mum, but Squirrel just snuggled under
the covers. "I don't like playing outside when it's cold," he moaned.
"Come on, it'll be fun," said Mum. Squirrel finally groaned and rolled out of bed.

"There are lots of interesting things to see when it's cold," said Mum.
She pointed to a row of icicles hanging from the windowsill.
Squirrel snapped one off and threw it through the air.
"It's like an ice rocket!" he said, as it landed with a crash on the path.

In the rose bushes, Squirrel noticed frosty cobwebs and
frozen raindrops hanging from the leaves. They sparkled
like diamonds in the sunlight. Squirrel was amazed.
"Everything looks so magical," he said, blowing on the
cobwebs so they glittered and glimmered.

"The grass is all spiky. It crunches when I walk on it," said Squirrel.
"That's because it's covered in frost," said Mum.
Squirrel ran round and round in circles, giggling to himself.
"Look, Mum," he said. "I'm making frost patterns on the grass!"

Squirrel scampered over to the pond. "Wow! It's frozen," he said.
He threw some little stones and they skidded across
the surface. Then, Squirrel dropped a big stone on the ice.
"Cool," gasped Squirrel, as it broke with a sharp crack.
"Look! The fish can come up for air now," said Squirrel's mother.

Squirrel's mother shivered. "I'm cold," she said. "I think it's time to go."
"Can I stay out longer, please Mum?" said Squirrel. "There's so much to see."
Squirrel's mother smiled. "I thought you didn't like playing out in the cold."
"I don't like it," said Squirrel, laughing. "I love it!"

Winter in the Garden

It was winter in the garden and Little Mouse was sad.
She missed the pretty flowers and the leaves the trees once had.

Her daddy knew just what to do. "I've got a plan," he said.
He twisted lights round branches and put lanterns by the shed.

"You will need a blanket," Daddy said, "and a hot drink from the house."
Little Mouse wondered why. "You'll see," said Daddy Mouse.

Outside was a crackling campfire and twinkling fairy lights.
"It's a magic garden!" cried Little Mouse, as she hugged her daddy tight.

Hide-and-Seek

Polar Bear was playing Hide-and-Seek with his friend, Brown Bear.
"You hide first," he said. "I'll count to ten. One, two, three, four, five."
Brown Bear dashed off and dived into a pile of brown leaves.

"Six, seven, eight, nine, ten. Coming, ready or not."
Polar Bear looked for a long time, but he couldn't find
Brown Bear anywhere. "Where are you?" he called.
"Boo! Here I am!" cried Brown Bear, jumping up.

Now it was Polar Bear's turn to hide. He scrambled under a big, green bush. Brown Bear finished counting and spotted her friend right away. "Found you!" she shouted. "That was too easy. You can have another turn."

Brown Bear shut her eyes and started counting again. Polar Bear
duck behind the garden shed and waited, keeping very still.
"I can see you already!" cried Brown Bear, pointing.
Polar Bear couldn't work out why he was so easy to find.
"It's because your fur is so white," said Brown Bear, giggling.

87

Polar Bear didn't want to play Hide-and-Seek any more.
He felt sad. He sat down under a tree and stared at his feet.
"What's the matter, Polar Bear?" asked Brown Bear, in a worried voice.

Before Polar Bear could answer, something cold dripped
on his nose. He looked up and saw that it was snowing!
Soon, the garden was covered in a blanket of snow.
Polar Bear had an idea. "Can I hide one more time?" he asked.

Polar Bear dived in the snow and lay down, carefully covering his black nose with a paw. He was very hard to spot because of his snow-white fur. Brown Bear looked everywhere for him. "I give up," she sighed at last.

When Polar Bear sprang out, Brown Bear was so surprised that she fell over. Her brown fur was covered in snow and she couldn't help laughing. "Now I'll be good at hiding in the snow, too," she said.

Raccoon's Winter Picnic

Raccoon and his friends had been playing in the snow all morning.
"I've made some sandwiches," called Raccoon's mother from the house.
"I'll take them in the garden and eat them later," said Raccoon.
"It's too cold to eat outside," his mother replied, but Raccoon wasn't listening.

In the garden, Raccoon said, "Let's build an igloo to eat our lunch in."
His friends made bricks out of snow and helped Raccoon pile them one on
top of the other. When the igloo was finished, the friends crawled inside.
Suddenly, they all felt very hungry.

Raccoon fetched the lunch and brought it inside the igloo.
"These sandwiches are frozen solid!" moaned Squirrel.
"This drink is so cold it's hurting my teeth!" complained Badger.
Raccoon and his friends were still very hungry.

Raccoon's mother looked out into the garden.
"Come into the house," she said. "I have a surprise for you."
She had made a fort out of blankets, chairs and cushions.
"Hooray!" shouted Raccoon and his friends, dashing inside.

95

"I think the best winter picnics are indoors," said Raccoon's mother, with a smile on her face. The friends scrambled under the blankets and found a new plate of sandwiches and drinks waiting for them.

"Thanks, Mum," said Raccoon, drinking his juice. "I think you are right."